CRAVING HER CURVES

CRAVING HER CURVES

A BBW ROMANCE

CARMEL EVANS

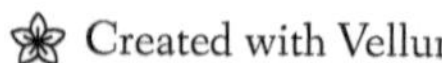 Created with Vellum

CONTENTS

1

ALISON

I've never cared about rugby league, yet here I am, in Barry's passenger seat as he drives me to the stadium, clipping and unclipping the lanyard on my media pass.

At least it's a good photo, I think ruefully—one of the perks of working for a national newspaper is access to great photographers. It's far better than the photo I had at my old job, a supermarket chain, where I had a blurry shot taken on my manager's phone when I wasn't quite ready. I used to hide that pass in my pocket until I needed to swipe it—but this one's nice enough to clip on the side of my bag, where the temptation to play with it is impossible to resist.

Of course, the fact that it annoys Barry doesn't hurt at all. He grunts as we approach the queue of cars at the gate and winds his window down.

'General admission?' the guy in the yellow vest asks.

'Media,' Barry says, holding up his pass. The man in. The vest doesn't ask for mine, although I've got it ready to hand over—he waves us through to a section of the parking area that's marked with blue witches hats instead of orange.

'Just stay behind me and keep quiet,' Barry says, as he manoeuvres the car into a spot on uneven ground. 'I'll ask all the questions.'

That's more than he said the entire drive and the resentment's clear in his voice. He's an old-school reporter with bloodshot eyes and thinning hair, someone who looks like he's spent thirty years pulling all-night stakeouts to be the first journalist on the scene, and resents anyone who uses the internet. He hates me because he hates everyone, but he's got a special level of resentment for female reporters at sporting matches.

It's just a few hours, I remind myself as I trudge after him, trying not to let my feet slip on the gravel, *and then he'll be someone else's problem.*

We reach the stadium entrance and instead of walking up to the queues, Barry goes straight to the security guard and shows him our passes. The guard's eyes flick up and down my dress, one of my favourites, a bright pink one that cradles my hips and breasts like it was sewn especially for me.

'Sign in here,' the guard says, nodding to a book inside the door, and I comply, writing my name and phone number in neat loopy handwriting. Barry's is more like chicken scratch that I can barely read, but the guard lets us in anyway.

Barry doesn't wait for me—he's already on the move and I jog to catch up.

'We'll interview Corey before the game,' he says, as he strides along the corridor. 'And again when it's done. I'll ask all the questions—all you need to do is stand behind me so Vivian can see you in the frame.' He glances back at me and I know he's thinking of his weekly shouting matches with

Vivian—he always closes her office door, but the walls are thin and the building's acoustics make their voices travel.

'Just send me by myself,' Barry usually says, 'I don't need to babysit anyone.'

'You know there's a focus on equal representation now,' Vivian replies, with an astonishing level of patience. 'We have to be seen to represent men and women equally at sporting matches or we'll get blasted on social media.'

'Who gives a shit,' Barry usually says, 'nobody takes that rubbish seriously, anyway.'

So far, I'd done a great job of staying out of 'that rubbish', but this week, Vivian chose me to be Barry's latest babysitting charge.

And nobody ever says no to Vivian. Not even Barry, despite his rants of protest.

He grudgingly marches me towards the throng of journalists who've already gathered to interview the captain of the North Sydney Chargers. They're clustered on the edge of the field, standing on the frost-capped grass, their cameras and microphones already assembled. We're not using a camera for this one—Vivian's already got a standing contract with one of the television networks—but I've got a microphone and voice recorder in my bag.

Barry takes his place in the crowd and takes the microphone without a 'thank you'. As instructed, I stand to the side and gaze up at the stadium as it slowly fills with people. The weather's brilliant and there are hardly any spare seats. Everyone's wearing red and black or blue and yellow, the colours of the teams playing today.

The reporters suddenly fall quiet and I can see why— the Chargers' captain jogs out of the stadium, his legs flexing beneath his red and black shorts, and stands there like being on national television is no scarier than standing in a queue at the bank.

Whenever I've seen football on TV, the players look like ants on the field. This man is so tall and broad he makes Barry look like a grey-haired child.

His amber eyes fall on me, and my breath catches.

He's the most gorgeous man I've ever seen.

My favourite coach taught me a valuable lesson: you're only as good as your most recent game. The worst thing you can do, he said, is reach the point where you think 'that's it, I've made it', because that's when you start losing everything you've worked for.

I'm thinking about that while I lace my shoes in the change room, pulling them tighter until there's no give left in them, and tying them in double knots. It's one of my pre-game rituals, and the worse I've been playing, the tighter my shoes need to be. The discomfort's my constant reminder to myself: *run faster, tackle harder, fight stronger*. We're playing the Queensland Colts today and the betting agencies say we're going to win, but I don't like to take anything for granted.

Especially when I made so many mistakes in our last game.

It was nothing major—we still won—but I had a few moments where I didn't play as well as I should have. Sure, after sixty consecutive matches I'm probably not as passionate about winning as I once was, but that's no excuse.

You're only as good as your most recent game.

I bounce from one foot to the other, like a boxer, testing the feel of my shoes. Around me, the other guys are going through their own pre-game rituals and the room smells like feet and deodorant.

'Are we ready, boys?' I boom.

'Hell yeah!' they say in unison. I walk around the room, giving them all high-fives. We've gone over our strategies so many times that they must know them better than their own names by now.

Ron, our coach, jogs into the room with a clipboard.

'Corey! The media's ready for you.'

I give the guys a final high-five and follow Ron out to the field. When I first started playing football, fresh out of high school, I felt like a superhero. But these days, there are parts of what I do that feel like a hard slog. Talking to the media's one of them—there's a crowd of crusty journalists who ask the same questions over and over, when all I want to do is get out there and play.

It's the same faces week after week—the same setup with cameras and boom mics and television station logos everywhere.

But this week, there's a new face. She's standing behind the other journalists in a pink dress, and I can't keep my eyes off her as I answer the same questions I'm always asked, while barely listening to what they say. Caramel hair tumbles over her shoulders, and her eyes are the colour of melted chocolate. Her dress accentuates her hourglass shape, and it's the first time I've ever been rendered speechless.

I trail off mid-answer. 'I'm sorry, what was the question again?'

The old reported sighs and I make a mental note to tie my shoes even tighter before kick-off.

3

____

ALISON

Fifteen minutes into the game, I still haven't written a single thing on my notepad.

Barry chews a stick of gum without offering me any. 'That's Corey,' he says, as the towering man we interviewed charges into the other team, running even after they tackle him, determined to keep going until they bring him to his knees. 'He's the team captain, but he's retiring at the end of this season.'

Corey rolls the ball under one foot and another player picks it up and throws it to another guy, who the blue and yellow team bring down straight away.

'Why's that?' I ask.

Barry's too absorbed in the game to mock my ignorance. His eyes flick back and forth, following the action on the field. The blue and yellow team have the ball now, but Corey's team's formed a human wall and they're not letting anyone through.

'He's had a few injuries,' he says, 'and he's old. He's been slowing down lately, but today he's on fire.'

Old? I shade my eyes with my hand. I would have thought he was thirty, maybe, but no older than that.

I'd ask what he means but Corey's got the ball again and Barry's on the edge of his seat, his legs trembling like he's about to spring up and leap over the temporary fence separating us from the field. He's shouting at the referee, but his raspy voice gets lost in all the other sounds in the stadium.

The players are getting dirty now, their shorts streaked with mud. The smell of hot chips and meat pies waft around us and I'm getting hungry, and I'd rather explore the rest of the stadium than stay with Barry for the next hour.

The pass in my handbag seems to open doors everywhere—why not see what's behind them?

'I'm going for a walk,' I say to Barry, but he ignores me.

THE STADIUM LOOKS simple when you're in the stands, but underneath, it's a labyrinth. I venture along a concrete tunnel that twists and turns, munching a sausage roll with tomato sauce that I bought at one of the crowded takeaway stalls.

This isn't so bad, I think. Sure, Barry's a crotchety old man, but what else would I be doing instead? I'd probably be working on some kind of feature article, even though it's Saturday. Everyone at the Southern Cross Gazette thinks I'm diligent and dedicated, but the truth is, I just don't want to be at home. Being there, alone, in the house I'd set up to raise a family in with my ex is far too painful.

Even working with Barry is better than staring at the empty space in my bed.

The further I walk, the fewer people I find. Eventually

there's hardly anyone at all and when I pass doors with nameplates that say 'stadium manager' and 'managing director', I know I'm deep inside the building.

There's sauce on my fingers, and I lick it off, but the stickiness remains. I look around for a bathroom—there's one not far down the corridor and I head for it. There's amplified giggling inside and I don't pay any attention until I hear the name 'Corey'.

I duck inside and find two cheerleaders leaning over the sinks to get a close-up view of their lips as they reapply lipstick. They're young—maybe twenty—and impossibly thin, so thin it's hard to imagine they're not missing a few internal organs. They don't notice me so I duck into a stall and press 'record' on my voice recorder, holding my breath as they keep gossiping.

'I can't believe she went out with him in the first place,' one of them says. 'Everyone knows Corey's a massive ladies' man.'

'And to dump her by text,' the cheerleader with the higher voice says. 'He hasn't changed at all, but Ashley brought it on herself.'

I wish I could rewind their conversation to hear the beginning of it. Are they talking about Corey, the football player we interviewed before the game? My heart sinks—I wouldn't have pegged him as being a sleaze, but I'm not that surprised. What else could I possibly expect, from someone who has access to as many models and cheerleaders as he wants?

A third voice joins them, a deeper female one.

'It's nearly half-time, come on.'

I hear makeup bags clasp and shuffling footsteps as the cheerleaders leave the bathroom, and wait until they're gone before unlatching the door. I rinse the sauce off my hand and stare at my reflection in the mirror that looks like it was cleaned with a muddy rag.

It feels strange to be let down by someone I've never even properly met, but at least I've got a story for Vivian.

4

___

COREY

Something's changed.

For the first time all season, I'm playing like a champion again.

It's her, I can feel it. The woman in the pink dress. She's out there in the crowd, and knowing that makes me feel like I'm doing this for a reason, for the first time since we lost last year's grand final.

Usually, when I play, I lose myself to the game and forget the spectators are even there. But today, every time there's a break, I find myself scanning the crowd, searching the blurred figures for glimpses of pink.

It's impossible, I know that. Trying to see an individual face in a stadium filled with thousands of people is like searching for a specific jigsaw puzzle piece in a freshly opened box.

Even though I can't see her, I know she's out there somewhere, and it drives me forward, makes me crave that winning trophy more than I have in months.

I score twice and when the other guys pat my back, I

feel like I should publicly dedicate our sudden turnaround to her.

But I can't.

That's the thing about being an athlete—everyone expects you to date cheerleaders and models. I've never liked them—I prefer women with more substance, someone who doesn't feel like they'll blow away in the wind. Women who'll go halves on a pizza without throwing up in the bathroom afterwards.

Women like the reporter in the pink dress.

But if I was to date someone like her, I think, as I dodge a would-be tackle, the other guys will be relentless. The media will drag her through the mud and make her life a living hell.

I can't do that to her.

Nevertheless, she's still on my mind when the timer ticks down to the last few seconds and the Colts have already given up. I can see it in their eyes, in the way they keep their heads down as their legs spin in the mud, not getting them any closer to the end of the field. The ball passes from one player to another, and every time, someone from my team blocks them.

Finally, the buzzer sounds. We shake hands with the other team, our muddy hands clasping in a show of team spirit, even though I can see the misery in the Colts' eyes. The trophy's ours, and today more than ever, I feel like we've really earned it.

But that's not what's really making me smile.

The media's already gathering and I know I'll get to see the woman in the pink dress again. I jog over, grinning like an idiot. Maybe after I've answered their questions and the TV guys disappear, I'll see if I can talk to her one-on-one.

The guys can't give me a hard time if they don't know what I'm doing.

But then, after all the usual questions have been asked, she steps forward.

'Corey,' she says, her voice clear. 'Can you tell us about your relationship with Ashley Parker?'

I blink, all the words knocked out of me.

How on earth did the reporter know about that?

5

———

ALISON

'You shouldn't have done that.' Barry glares at the road as he drives, but it's clear from the tone of his voice that he'd rather be directing that glare at me. 'I told you not to say anything, and what do you do?' He flicks the blinker angrily, and it makes a ticking sound.

'It's a great story,' I say, but the criticism still burns.

'It's gossip,' Barry mutters. 'That's Corey Aldridge, not some chick on the cooking channel.' He turns into our office building and shakes his head. 'All you needed to do was stand there and be quiet, and you had to open your big mouth.'

Of course I did—I'm a reporter—but working here has taught me to pick my battles, so I stay quiet.

Vivian isn't much better. When we report back to her office, she's holding a printout of my email and seems less enthusiastic than I'd expected.

'Footballer beds cheerleader?' she says, tapping the end of her pen against her notebook. 'That's not really a new angle, is it?'

Barry looks gleeful for the first time today and I realise

he looks like a weasel when he smiles. I stare at the floor to avoid looking at him. How could I possibly describe everything I felt in the bathroom, how this information hit me like a punch in the gut? In the moment, it felt like a massive scandal but now, in Vivian's office, I can see how unremarkable it must look to an editor.

'Call the cheerleader and see if she'll give you an interview,' Vivian sighs, passing the email to me. 'Nobody's gonna read it, but we need to publish something.'

I THOUGHT that would be the end of it—that I'd publish the article, a different female reporter would be sent to work with Barry and I'd be reassigned to my usual role.

But a week later, Vivian appears at my desk while I'm typing, her face red and her nostrils flaring.

'What is it?' I ask, my fingers freezing mid-word.

'Corey's here,' she says.

'Corey?' I feel like there's a stone sinking in my stomach. When I called Ashley, she told me everything about their date in great detail and I published the whole thing. Corey must have read it, and he must have really hated it to have come all the way here. I glance across the office to the interview room where, sure enough, there's Corey's strong and unmistakable silhouette.

'I'll get Barry,' I say, but Vivian blocks my path as I stand up.

'He's not here for Barry.' She stares at me, and I feel like her eyes are drilling through my skull. 'He specifically asked to see you.'

6

———

COREY

W hat am I doing? You'd think I'd know better than to jeopardise my entire career like this, but maybe I don't. Because even though I know I shouldn't pursue Alison, I'm still driving into her office feeling like a schoolboy who's about to ask a girl to the year twelve formal.

Except in this case, it's no girl.

Alison Turner is all woman, and it's been years since I've been unable to get someone out of my head like this. After she left, I checked the media sign-in sheets and found her name beneath the old guy she was there with. Her name, her phone number and the name of the newspaper she works for.

It's a tiny publication I've never heard of, the Southern Cross Gazette, but the building's big enough, marked with a sign across its facade that I must have ignored a hundred times as I've driven past. A security guard points to the sign-in sheet and his eyes widen when I'm halfway through writing my name.

'Corey Aldridge?' he gasps. He's a solid guy who looks

like he might have been a regular footy player himself, before middle-age spread and grey hair took over.

'That's me,' I say.

'Seriously?' The guy's face breaks into a smile. '*The* Corey Aldridge? You're a legend!'

'That's what they tell me,' I say, although it isn't how I feel right now, especially after reading Alison's article. I feel like Corey Aldridge: failed footballer and womanising jerk.

But as character-destroying as that article was, it gave me an idea. Maybe if I spoke to Alison and agreed to tell my side of the story, she'd spend some time with me, one-on-one.

And if it's for work, nobody can give either of us a hard time.

'Who are you here to see?' the guard asks, and I hesitate. I don't want to give him Alison's name—what if he calls her and she refuses to come down?

'Barry Kerr,' I say, remembering the name above hers on the sign-in sheet.

'I'll call him down,' the guard says, taking the clipboard from me and handing me a visitor's pass. 'Take a seat.'

7

―――――――

ALISON

I've interviewed politicians and rock stars, and I've never felt as star-struck as when I stand outside the interview room with my hand on the doorknob, trying to get my nerves under control.

Why does Corey want to see me? Does he hate the article? Is he going to rip me to shreds?

There's only one way to find out. I steel myself and twist the door handle. There he is, sitting at the desk where Vivian's left a glass of water, so massive he makes our furniture look like it belongs in a doll's house. He's even more gorgeous close-up and when he's not covered in mud—his stubble's just the right length to make him look rugged, without looking scruffy, and his jeans and shirt are the perfect blend of casual and hot.

And then there are those eyes.

I feel like they're looking directly into my soul.

'What can I do for you?' I ask, trying to ignore my heart as it hammers against my ribcage.

'Alison, is it?' The way Corey says my name makes my

19

stomach lurch. I stay as still as I can so he can't see my trembling hands.

'Yes, that's me.'

Corey rests his hands on the table. They're enormous—that's the first thing I notice. They look big enough to pick up a watermelon as though it's a tennis ball. I swallow, trying not to imagine how those fingers might feel inside me.

He's a player, I warn myself.

'I don't usually do this,' he says without smiling, and my stomach sinks. This is it, the moment he rips me apart. I brace myself for the first blow, not expecting what he says next. 'I'm here to ask a favour. A really big one.'

I hold my breath. What could Corey Aldridge possibly want from me? He's a well-known football player and I'm a reporter for a small newspaper. Our worlds aren't even in the same universe, let alone the same orbit.

Corey watches me with a steady gaze. 'I want you to write my biography.'

I blink, not sure I heard him right. 'What?'

'My biography,' Corey repeats. 'I want you to tail me for the rest of the season and write a book about me. This'll be my last season and I want to make the most of it while I can.'

I feel my mouth open and close as I wonder why he's speaking to me, the woman with no interest in football who wrote a scathing piece about him last week.

'Barry's our sports reporter,' I say. 'I'll send him in. He's written a few biographies before, mostly for cricketers, but I'm sure he'll love to help you.'

Corey reaches out and touches my wrist. The heat from his fingers radiates through my skin.

'It has to be you,' he says.

'Why me?' I say, confused. 'I'm not a sports reporter.'

'You're my good luck charm,' he says, looking away like he's revealing a deep hidden secret. 'I played my best game this season last week—and this week, I could barely hold the ball.' He looks at me pleadingly. 'Please say yes.'

I hesitate. On the one hand, I was so happy to get away from covering football.

But on the other, having an excuse to see Corey every day would make my job a lot more pleasant.

'Okay,' I say, but as Corey smiles and shakes my hand, a new feeling of dread sets in.

I've never written a book before, and even though I don't exactly have anyone waiting for me at home, it'll mean a lot of extra time at the office.

What am I getting myself into?

COREY

She said yes!

The biography was a last-minute idea I had in the elevator, and I wasn't even sure I'd go with it until it popped out of my mouth.

It was Alison who changed my mind. Seeing her and speaking to her, so close I could see her chest rise and fall as she breathed. The woman who wasn't afraid to ask difficult questions and who spurred me into playing the best game of my life.

I had to get to know her.

A feature article wouldn't give us much time together, I reasoned—and while I've got no doubt I could bed a cheerleader in an hour, I figured I'd need more time than that for someone like Alison, who wouldn't just fawn over me just because I'm a footy player.

The only catch? The book deal doesn't exist.

Back in my car, I think through every conversation I've had with my manager, searching my memory for any mention of books. Finding nothing, I call him as I drive.

'Jase, do you know if there's been any offers to publish a biography about me?'

He's quiet for a moment, and then I hear his voice, muffled like he's talking to someone else.

'I haven't heard anything,' he says, coming back to the phone. 'But leave it with me and I'll do some sniffing around. I've got a mate at Caret Publishing—maybe he can help out.'

'Thanks Jase,' I say, but when I hang up, I don't feel any better. Sure, I've got a good reason for Alison to come to my house now, but how's she going to feel when she finds out there isn't a deal in place?

Tess, my kelpie, hears me coming and barks as I pull into the driveway, and when I open the gates, she hurls herself into the passenger seat and looks ecstatic to be driven up to the house. She was a stray I found in a box on the side of the road—someone had obviously dumped her, and I couldn't resist bringing her home. Since then, she's been the best friend I could possibly have.

I make my way down to the workshop beneath the house, with Tess following me. I've been slowly building an ornate king-sized bed that I'll eventually sleep in. It's something I only work on every now and then, usually when I need to take my mind off something, so it's covered with spiderwebs that I brush off with a wave of my hand. I read somewhere that spiders' webs are stronger than steel, but these ones break apart with the slightest touch.

An hour disappears into sanding and sawing, and I only stop working when the sunlight disappears and the overhead lights cast shadows over the parts I'm working on.

My back cracks as I stretch it and reach for my phone. There's a message from Alison: *I've been thinking about the book. Do you mind if I pop over and talk to you soon?*

9

———

ALISON

I don't know what's gotten into me. Ever since Corey's asked me to write his book, he's all I've been able to think about. His arms, his eyes, his muscles... I've been unable to concentrate at work and at night, in bed, I fantasise about him touching my hand while I reach beneath the sheets and play with myself.

I feel like I'm at the beginning of a new adventure, and I can't wait to see where it leads.

———

Those butterflies only grow stronger as I drive to Corey's house. He lives just out of Sydney, in an area that feels like it belongs on a postcard. There are *cows*, of all things, and ducks that stand on the gravel road until I drive right up to them.

This is definitely not the kind of place I expected a football player to live.

The first sign that someone important lives here are the solid gates across his driveway. I press the intercom button and wait, my heart pounding. This isn't like me at all, and I swallow in a vain attempt to minimise my nervousness.

He's just a person, I remind myself. A rich, hot, athletic male person, who makes my pussy throb every time I think about him.

Finally, the speaker crackles to life.

'Alison? Come on in.'

I'm not sure where he wants me to park, so I follow the driveway around as the gates swing closed behind me. A brown kelpie runs out from behind the house, tail wagging, and I slow right down so I don't hit it.

'Tess!' Corey shouts, jogging after her. 'Sorry, she's hopeless.'

As soon as I open my door she's up, paws on my leg, trying to lick me. Corey grabs her collar and pulls her back, and I try to look graceful as I climb out of the car in a skirt that pulls my knees together.

Not the best choice, in hindsight, but his eyes scan my legs and warmth rushes through my abdomen.

'You've got a beautiful property,' I say, shading my eyes to get a good view of the sloping landscape and the tree-lined valley. It would be a great spot for a wedding, I think, but don't say.

He watches me but I'm too scared to look into his eyes just yet, afraid I might tumble into them and blurt out everything I'm feeling. Which, right now, is a combination of confused, nervous, aroused and excited. I want to fall into his arms and kiss him, but instead I clear my throat.

'Shall we go inside?'

'Sure.' Corey leads me into the house and, walking behind him, I can't help but notice the easy way his body moves in his casual clothes, and the strength in his ass beneath his shorts. Tess bounds in ahead of us as soon as he opens the door, but I wait until he gestures for me to go in.

Everything within the house is just as beautiful as everything outside it. There's wooden floorboards and furniture, which gives the whole place a treehouse vibe, but his football trophies, wine collection and new kitchen make it feel like it was decorated for an interior design magazine.

The only room that looks out-of-place is his bedroom, with its do-it-yourself bedframe and black blanket, although he closes the door before I can get a good look at it.

How many cheerleaders have been in there, I wonder.

I sit on the leather couch and pick up a carved wooden figurine from the side table. It's beautiful and ornate, but I can't tell what it's supposed to be.

'What's this?' I ask.

'Just something I made,' Corey says, as he sits on the other couch, one leg across the other. 'Woodwork's my other passion. I've got a workshop downstairs.'

Now when I look at him again, I notice sawdust on his shirt and callouses on his giant fingers.

'Do you think you'll work as a builder after your football career finishes?' I ask, completely disregarding all the carefully written questions in the folder I brought with me.

Corey shrugs. 'Maybe. I don't really know what I'm gonna do, to be honest. My life's always revolved around football.' He scratches his leg. 'I guess I never expected to be single at this stage of my career—I always expected to be married by now, maybe a couple of kids. But I guess I've just been unlucky.'

His eyes meet mine and despite the quickly plummeting temperature, the room feels ten degrees warmer. I'm itching to ask the questions I really want to know the answers to: *Have you ever been married? Why are you single? Could you ever be attracted to me?* but instead, I open my folder and scan my typed list of questions.

Question one: how did you start playing football?

That seems like a safe place to begin.

10
———

COREY

I can't believe she's in my house.

Alison's sitting there with her shoes off and her feet curled under her, like she's hanging out with her best friend, and I'm letting my entire life fall out of my mouth.

Man, I'm nervous. Jase still hasn't found a publisher who's willing to print my biography and I hate lying to her, but what will happen if I tell her about that now?

I don't want her to know I lied. But more than anything, I don't want her to leave.

I tell her about my childhood, my football trophies, the scar on my shoulder. She only needs to ask the occasional question as I find more tangents to dip down, more insignificant moments I haven't thought about in years that suddenly seem meaningful in her presence.

'Do you mind if I speak with other people in your family and team, too?' she asks, and I hesitate.

This is the most I've ever told anyone about my life. Later, she'll interview guys who've known me my entire life, and they'll all tell her the same thing—that I'm stoic, reserved, a man of few words—and she won't recognise the version of me that they describe.

It's like I can feel completely free with her, like all my normal boundaries have fallen away.

It's getting dark again—it always feels like it's getting dark at this time of year—and when she curls her feet higher under her body, I realise she must be cold.

'Shit,' I say, halfway through a story about my first tryout for the Chargers. 'You must be cold.'

'It's okay,' she says, but I'm already up, stacking wood in the antique fireplace that, along with the solitude, was my main reason for buying this house. All I want to do is impress her, and for the first time in ages, I feel like my tattoos and football trophies aren't going to get me there.

She's looking at my trophy cabinet now, her eyes scanning the engraved plates: most points in a season, most tries, highest score. I've even still got my tarnished old trophies from when I was a kid, on the bottom shelf: most improved, best and fairest, and the ever-ubiquitous participation ribbons.

'We train in all sorts of weather,' I say apologetically, 'so I've stopped noticing the cold so much.'

Smoke curls up as soon as I touch the firelighter to the wood, and soon there's a comforting blaze that warms the air around us.

'Would you like some more wine?' I ask, and she nods. She's kneeling in front of the trophy cabinet, inspecting the oldest ones, the firelight flickering over her curves.

I pour two glasses and bring them back to the couch.

She moves on from the trophy cabinets, perusing the decorative carving that I made from an old teak table.

'You're really good at this,' she murmurs, as she runs her finger over the wood. 'What else have you made?'

'This table,' I say, nudging the coffee table with my foot. 'That bookcase over there. Pretty much everything you see that's made out of wood.'

'I'd love to see more of your work,' she says, as she surveys me over the glass. Her chocolate eyes pull me in and I feel like I'm completely under her spell.

'Would you like to see my workshop?' I ask, before I can stop myself.

ALISON

Corey's workshop is underneath his house and we have to make our way down a winding outdoor staircase to get there. The wood's uneven from years of exposure to the elements and he goes down first, stepping carefully, guiding me whenever we reach a wonky plank.

As we reach the last few steps, I realise that the lower half of the house has a long glass wall and overlooks the valley, although all I can see out there now is an inky blackness. Corey slides the door open and we step onto a concrete door covered with sawdust and, when he flicks the lights on, I notice we're in a massive room that looks and smells like a carpenter's workshop. The three walls are lined with workbenches and there's equipment that looks vaguely familiar from my high school woodworking classes.

The middle of the room is filled by a half-built bed. It has to be bigger than king-size, when you take all the decorative carvings into account, and as I drag my hand over the intricate details, I can't help but gasp.

'What do you think?' Corey asks, as I slowly walk around it.

'It looks like something from a fairytale,' I breathe. My fingers snare on something sticky and I jump, colliding with Corey.

'Was that a spider?'

'It's covered with cobwebs,' Corey says, brushing the silk off my fingers. 'I haven't worked on it much this year—training's been too intense.'

Our bodies are close. I can feel the heat from his chest radiating through my arm and I can feel his breath in my hair. It's turning me on so much that my brain feels like it's melting—and that's never a good thing for a journalist, let alone a woman who's standing in front of a man with a proven bad reputation.

Still, all I want to do is fall into his giant arms.

He's so tall that I could easily nuzzle my head against his chest and feel safe and secure forever.

For a second, I think he feels the same way, but then he picks up a piece of sandpaper and runs it over a rough piece in the wood.

'When are you planning to finish it?'

'Whenever it's done.' Corey looks thoughtful. 'My whole life is monitored, measured and evaluated. This is something that's just for me, that I can finish whenever I like. It's the only time the clock's not ticking.'

Our eyes meet again and, this time, there's no way I'm imagining it. There's electricity there, and sadness in his eyes too.

I reach down and squeeze his hand.

12

COREY

My pulse thuds in my ears as our lips meet. It's like nothing I've ever felt before—it's like we're at the centre of the universe and the stars are soaring around us.

I reach behind her back and pull her close to me, and I know she can feel my erection through my pants. It seems to make her hungrier, to kiss me with less self-consciousness, and it's the hottest thing in the world.

'Let's go back upstairs,' I say, taking her hand. 'It's warmer there.'

My steel-framed bed is terrible in comparison to this one, but at least there's a mattress on it. And it's in the bedroom, rather than a workshop in full view of anyone who might live within thirty kilometres.

I gently tug Alison's hand but, to my surprise, she doesn't follow me.

I turn back, confused. Alison's looking at the ground now, her eyes wet.

'What is it?'

She blinks. 'I really want to...' her voice wavers, 'but I

know how you treat women. I don't want to be another notch on your bedpost.'

The question that she asked at the football match comes back to me.

'Where did you hear about Ashley Parker?'

Alison's eyes drop. 'I overheard two cheerleaders talking in the bathroom, and then I found her on the internet. If you can treat a cheerleader like that, I can only imagine how you'd treat me...'

I'm stunned. How could she possibly think there's any comparison?

I sit on the side of the bed frame and hold Alison's hand between both of mine.

'I only went out with Ashley once,' I explain. 'She was never my girlfriend, her friends made her think there was more between us than there really was. She got drunk and spent three hours talking about her chihuahua, and when I dropped her home, she dangled over the handrail and begged me to come inside. And then threw up on a rose bush.'

Alison chuckles. 'I can see how that might be painful.'

I nod solemnly. 'The dog's name was Sir Bigglesworth.'

Alison bursts out laughing, and I'm relieved that at least she doesn't hate me. 'Still,' she says, 'you're a footballer. Footballers go out with cheerleaders. Not...' she pauses, and I want to finish that sentence for her. *Gorgeous women? Women of substance?* 'People like me,' she says flatly.

'You're a thousand times better than a cheerleader,' I say, pulling her close enough for her to feel the heat between my legs. 'And I'm sick of worrying about what the other guys might think. Or the media. I'm just worried about how they'll treat you.'

My lips find hers again and, this time, she doesn't resist.

'Well, I am the media,' she says, as my rock-hard cock twitches with happy anticipation. 'And I say, bring it on.'

35

ALISON

Corey throws me on the bed and my heart races as our lips move against each other and my pussy throbs with excitement.

His bedroom is definitely different to the rest of the house—there's hardly anything personal in here, just the steel-framed bed, a built-in wardrobe and a stack of clothes in the corner, red and black stripes visible among the rumble of colours. It feels like a room he doesn't spend much time in.

Maybe I can change that for him.

'You're so gorgeous,' he says, and his deep voice fills me with a rumbling desire that starts deep inside me.

'Look who's talking,' I tease, stroking his strong ass, feeling the muscles clench. Those eyes, that jawline, that full head of hair that feels as soft as it looks when I run my hand through it.

Even just looking at him makes me wet, and when his kisses trail down my body, towards the aching point between my legs, I know I've found the man of my dreams.

Every man I've ever been with before has been too

impatient to go down on me, so it's a delicious surprise when I feel Corey's scorching hot tongue on my clit. He rolls it around, teasing me, warming me up. Not that I need it, of course.

Ever since we spoke, I've been fantasising about him touching me, just like he is now, and all I want is for him to be inside me.

His tongue whirs faster, and I grab my breasts, squeezing them as pleasure jolts through my abdomen.

'Oh Corey,' I moan, as he strokes my wetness with his finger. 'That feels incredible.'

I can tell he's smiling by the way his cheeks move against my thighs, but he keeps going, like he's on a mission to give me the best orgasm of my life, slurping at my clit like it's made from honey.

Pleasure builds inside me and I arch my back as he slides a finger deep inside my pussy. My body accepts it hungrily, giving him no resistance, and he adds a second one. I'm so wet that there's a squelching sound as he moves them in and out, and I gasp as I realise how incredible his cock will feel after this.

I squeeze my breasts as my orgasm builds, my head rolling back and my heart races. His fingers slide in and out of me at the perfect speed, massaging my g-spot and tormenting my quivering clit.

'That's it,' he murmurs, as he pulls away to focus on his fingers for a moment. 'Come for me, gorgeous.'

I want to give him everything he needs. I look deep into his intense amber eyes as he grins and moves his fingers faster inside my pussy and over my clit, playing me like I'm a musical instrument.

'That's it, gorgeous,' he says, leaning over me so he can watch my face as I come.

Normally I'm self-conscious about anyone seeing me at such a private moment, but with Corey, I only feel that we're exactly where we're meant to be. My body lets go and I'm overtaken by a wave of pleasure, crying out as my pussy clenches around his fingers so tightly it must be hurting him, but he looks thrilled.

'Corey, I love you,' I pant without thinking, and then freeze. What am I doing? I can't say that! Not to someone like him, and certainly not before he says it first!

But to my relief, he smiles and kisses me.

'I love you too, gorgeous.'

14

———

COREY

She loves me!

Alison said she loves me!

My excitement intensifies as the full magnitude of this moment hits me. After feeling like I've reached the end of my potential ever since I decided to retire from the game, suddenly I feel like I've got something to live for again.

Especially when she's lying naked in front of me, her face flushed with pleasure and her legs wide open, revealing her warm wet opening, inviting me in.

My erection's rock hard and I rub the tip against her wetness, making her moan.

When I slide my cock inside her, I feel like I'm in heaven.

'I love you,' I say again, enjoying how the words feel in my mouth. 'I love you and I want to marry you, so I can be with you forever.'

I roll my hips, gliding in and out of her while my abs slide over her deliciously soft flesh. She kisses me, moaning into my mouth, and squeezes my butt, pulling me further inside.

'I want to be with you forever too,' she murmurs, her eyes full of lust. 'I want to do this every single day for the rest of my life.'

Nothing would make me happier. I thrust faster, plunging into her depths and she squeezes my back and her gasps tell me she's close again.

'All I want,' I whisper, as her pussy clenches around my cock, 'is to make you happy. Forever.'

Alison's body takes over, her eyes roll back in her head and her pussy grips my cock like a vice, milking it as she moans.

I can't hold back either—my cock explodes, filling her with my hot seed, twitching and throbbing until it's empty.

We lie there together in each other's arms, her head nuzzled against my chest as my cock softens inside her.

'Do you still believe I'm your good luck charm?' she asks, as she strokes my chest hair.

'A hundred percent,' I say.

'I think I do too,' she says, her restful face glowing with happiness. 'Because I can't figure out how else I'd get to be this lucky.'

I kiss her forehead and the pull of sleep becomes stronger. My eyelids droop and I know we'll both be asleep in five minutes.

'Me too,' I murmur, as I pull my arms more tightly around her.

15

———

ALISON

Everything is beautiful.

There's frost on the grass, rays of sunlight streaming through tufts of cloud, winter trees standing stoic against the brisk wind. But tiny leaves are also beginning to form, buds that are still tightly rolled, tiny signs that spring is on its way.

Even the Southern Cross Gazette building looks beautiful, despite its brutalist architecture. I say a cheery 'good morning' to the security guard who looks up in surprise as I saunter past in my brightest yellow dress.

Corey Aldridge loves me, I love him, and nothing could dull my happiness.

Not the anaemic office lights, not the expired milk in the fridge, not the note on my desk written in Vivian's sloped handwriting.

See me as soon as you get here.

I roll my eyes. This isn't what I want to deal with today —hopefully it's just a quick 'How's your book going?' and the hardest part will be trying not to blurt out, 'He loves me!'

But I know Vivian better than that.

Barry's in there too and there's a sparkle in his eye that makes him nervous.

'Take a seat,' Vivian says, which instantly takes the sunshine out of the room. 'Thanks for sending your interview notes in.' She pauses and I wait for whatever it is her insincere compliment's leading into. 'We did some research of our own, and when Barry called the publishing house...'

She glances at Barry, who by this point looks as gleeful as a cartoon supervillain.

'They've never heard of the book,' he says. 'And the general editor certainly didn't approve you to write it. They've got their own writers on staff—they almost never hire freelancers.'

I'm confused. What's going on? Who's lying—Corey or Barry?

Did Corey lie when he told me he loved me, too?

Luckily, my inner journalist is a step ahead of my inner frightened woman.

'I'll call them,' I say. 'I'm sure there's just been some miscommunication somewhere.'

Back at my desk, out of Barry's earshot, I dial the publishing house's number with a shaking finger.

'Hello?' a woman's voice says.

'Hi,' I say, imitating Vivian's stilted voice as best I can, not wanting to be fobbed off to some intern. 'I'm Vivian Anderson, the editor of the Southern Cross Gazette. Is the general editor...' I run my finger down my screen to find his name, 'Pete Goodacre available?'

There's some rustling and muffled voices on the other end of the phone, and then the sound of a man clearing his throat.

'Good morning, this is Pete Goodacre,' he says.

'Hi Pete,' I say in my sweetest voice. 'I'm Vivian from the Southern Cross Gazette, and I'd like to talk about your planned biography about Corey Aldridge.'

Pete clears his throat again. 'Look, we don't have anything planned. His manager called about it last week, but our publishing schedule's already full for the next two years.'

I don't know what to say. There's another voice on the other end of the phone and Pete says, 'If that's all, I've got a meeting to get to.'

'Thanks for your time,' I say in my sunniest voice, even though my heart's breaking inside.

16

COREY

This might be the happiest I've ever been.

There's all the obvious moments where I've been happy—my first professional game, my first grand final win... but nothing compares to happy I feel to know that Alison's mine.

It's like I've suddenly found the part of myself that was missing.

I work happily on the bed all morning, humming as I carve, imagining us lying on it, fucking on it, waking up glowing in each other's arms after a long night of sex.

Now that I've tasted her, I want more.

Much more.

My final game's coming up soon, and I've decided to propose to her in the middle of the stadium, in front of everyone. Down on one knee in the middle of the field, right under the setting sun. A quick chat to the sound guys will send a blast of her favourite song out around everyone right as I walk out with the ring tucked safely in my fist and a stupid big grin on my face.

To hell with what everyone else thinks, I think as I tap my chisel with a small hammer. *I want everyone to know that I love Alison Turner.*

I can already imagine it—the hush in the crowd as they realise what I'm doing, the collective holding of breath, seagulls squawking somewhere in the distance as I kneel in front of Alison and open the box with trembling fingers.

I've already got the ring—a princess-cut diamond in white gold, safely tucked away in its navy blue box.

I don't even know if she'll say yes, but this is something I have to do.

Being an athlete has taught me how to persevere even when things get hard.

This is a risk I have to take.

I'M SO ABSORBED in carving and sanding that I don't hear my phone beep, but when I take a break, pulling my shirt off so the sawdust doesn't keep prickling my skin, I pick up my phone and realise I've got twenty new messages.

Alison.

I smile, my heart doing happy flips to hear from her, but when I read her messages, my heart becomes a lead weight.

I called Caret Publishing, and they said there's no book deal.

What's going on?

Corey, are you avoiding me?

I close my eyes, unsure where to even start. All I know is that I don't want to wreck this, and I don't want to break her trust. But how can I, when I've already lied?

If only I'd already had a book deal in place. If only I'd

run it by them first before I'd approached Alison—I was just so keen to see her that I didn't think it through.

I slide the door open, hoping the fresh air will give me some ideas, but as I climb the stairs, I realise there's someone already up there, standing with their arms folded.

Alison.

17

ALISON

Is this a footballer thing, I wonder, as I drive way too fast. Is this the adult version of that old high school trick, leading the fat girl on just so you can make fun of her?

Maybe I took that last corner too fast, but my blood's boiling in my veins. I really thought he liked me—I thought he was attracted to me—but now I feel like an idiot for believing him.

Did he just want to get me into bed this entire time?

I press the buzzer at the gate twice, and he doesn't appear. He hasn't replied to any of my messages either— they're still marked as unread.

Is he ghosting me?

Is this what he did to Ashley?

I climb out of the car and survey the fence. It's pretty solid, but I've always been good at climbing and I scale it without any problem, dropping to the other side like a ninja, wincing at the pain that shoots through my ankle.

That's a problem for later.

It's good enough to walk on for now, so I make my way

down to his house. It looks quiet, but his car's there, so I know he's not far away. I knock on the front door and wait—no response.

He's definitely ghosting me, I think, and imagine the stories he'll tell women in the future: *we just had one date; it wasn't even a date, but she thought it was more. She said I love you the first time we had sex—can you imagine?*

I'm about to turn around when I realise Tess isn't barking. If he was inside the door, watching me through the peephole, wouldn't she have barked when I knocked?

Maybe he's downstairs in the workshop, I think, and for the first time all morning, I start to think that maybe he's not avoiding me after all. Maybe he's working with music playing, his phone on the bench to keep it safe.

I make my way around the house to those rickety steps and that's when I see him trudging up the stairs.

He's shirtless, and the sunlight makes his abs look like they're rippling.

Something inside me melts, but I remind myself why I'm here.

'Alison,' he says, pulling me into a hug that I don't return. 'I'm so glad you came to talk.'

His touch makes my body ache for him. The smell of sawdust and masculine energy is intoxicating, but I stay strong.

'Why did you like to me?' I ask, trying not to let my voice quiver. 'You made me look like an idiot in front of my boss.'

Tess trots up to us, and Corey pats her.

'I wanted an excuse to see you,' he admitted. 'You were so beautiful, so fiery... I needed to get to know you.'

'Why didn't you just say that then?' I sit on the step,

staring out over the valley. It's so picturesque and beautiful, and when I remember how I felt walking out into the sunshine this morning, it brings goosebumps to my arms.

Corey sits next to me, his shoulder pressed against mine. His skin's hot, his pulse is strong and all I want to do is kiss him again.

'I don't know,' he says, not looking at me. 'It was a spur-of-the-moment idea, and I thought for sure the publishing house would pick it up.'

I move my leg away from him. And in the meantime, you were gonna let me do hours of work for no reason?'

Corey smiles. 'Not exactly no reason. Wait here.'

He disappears inside the house and I fight the urge to follow him. When he comes back, he sits next to me again and hands me a slip of paper.

'What's this?' I ask, taking it from him.

'Payment,' he says, 'Everything upfront, so you know it's not a waste of time.'

I unfold the page—it's a cheque for a number far bigger than I've seen in my entire career.

'You're paying me for... sex?' I ask, not knowing whether to laugh or punch him.

'No!' Corey points to the description. 'For your work on the biography. Which I still want to write, by the way.'

'Even with no publishing deal?' I ask, wondering why he'd bother. 'There are cheaper ways to get to know me, you know.'

'I know.' Corey tilts his head and smiles, and it's almost impossible to resist him while he's gazing at me so intimately. 'I figure I'll probably have kids one day, and if a publishing house doesn't pick it up, I'll write it for them. Print it myself, if I have to.'

Dammit, there goes the last of my self-control. Corey gazes out into the valley, sunlight playing on his eyes, and I stroke his cheek until he turns around and gazes directly at me.

Our lips meet and I feel like I've come home.

18
____

COREY

Alison's hand's hot in mine as I lead her inside. We fall on the couch together and I claw at her top, desperate to touch her milky flesh, and she unhooks her bra with that delicious smile that tells me she knows exactly how much I love it.

I'm hard as a rock and there's no hiding it, especially when her hands explore my thighs, pulling my pants down, and those ruby lips touch the head.

Fire burns through my groin as she parts her lips, taking me inside her soft wet mouth. I feel like I'm about to come here and now, especially when she reaches under my balls, but I hold it back.

Seeing her in front of me, kneeling over my cock, her mouth pumping up and down while her naked body's right there, within my reach, is the hottest thing I've ever seen. I stroke her hair and watch her eyes close with pleasure as I caress her earlobe.

Alison's good at this.

Her eyes meet mine again as her tongue flicks over my

head as though she's licking melted ice-cream, and I can't take any more teasing.

I need to fuck her.

She pulls away when I touch her shoulder, as though she knows exactly how I'm feeling, and I press my lips against hers.

'I want you so bad,' I murmur. 'I want to fuck you until you're mine.'

I reach between her legs, feeling the delicious warmth between them. When I slide my fingers in, her pussy pulses around them, and when I pull them out, they're slick with her wetness.

The desire in her eyes confirms what her body already told me.

'I want to fuck you too,' she whispers. 'I want you deep inside me.'

I nudge the tip of my cock against her opening and she gasps as she tries to bear down on it. But I pull back, teasing her now, making her want it as much as I do.

If that's even possible.

At last, when neither of us can hold off any longer, I plunge my cock inside her, watching her eyes lose focus with pleasure.

'Come for me, gorgeous,' I pant, as I drive myself deeper inside her scorching hot pussy. Her clit stiffens against my pelvis and her breasts bounce as her face turns pink. 'Come for me, Alison.'

She doesn't need another invitation. Her eyes squeeze shut as her fingers tighten around my shoulders and her pussy throbs around my cock.

I'm deep inside her, my erection trapped against her cervix, and I kiss her parting lips as my cock erupts inside her.

We stay on the couch, lying squashed against each other in a sweaty haze of satisfaction. It's perfect... or would be, except that Tess starts to whine and scratch Alison's arm.

'Go away,' I mutter, swatting the air over the edge of the couch. Tess whines again and nudges my hand with her wet nose.

'What have you got there?' Alison asks, rolling over to inspect the object Tess dropped on the floor. I roll my eyes—it's probably one of her toys.

But Alison holds up a small navy blue box and looks questioningly at me.

'Shit,' I say. 'Tess, where'd you get that?'

It's the jewellery box that holds the engagement ring I'd planned to give her at my final match, intact aside from two incisor dents.

Why not, I think, looking at Alison's beautiful glowing face. It's not what I planned, but then again, none of this is. And it's still absolutely perfect.

'Alison Turner,' I say, climbing over her to kneel naked on the carpet next to the couch. 'Will you marry me?'

Alison squeals as I pull the box open.

19

ALISON

I t's Corey's last grand final.

The atmosphere's contagious and I'm dressed head-to-toe in red and black, shouting just as loud as everyone else, the gorgeous ring on my finger shimmering in the sunlight.

I still don't know much about football, but I love watching Corey's legs pump as he runs, and the ecstasy on his face at just being on the field.

Of course, I'd like to think I've got something to do with that, too. His eyes keep glancing back to me and I remember what he said about me being his good luck charm—since we've been together, his team hasn't lost a single game.

'Go Corey!' I scream, as the other team fumbles with the ball and Corey swoops in out of nowhere to grab it. Everyone around me turns to stare, but I don't let it bother me—my favourite team's winning and I'm in love.

Finally, the timer reaches two minutes, and Corey's got the ball.

The Chargers are safely ahead, but how amazing would

it be if Corey scored the last try in the last game of his career?

My heart's in my throat as he sprints up the field, the other players who try to tackle him falling away as though Corey's being protected by some invisible force.

The timer's down to 1:32 as he zigs and zags, dodging would-be opponents to make his way down the field.

Maybe the other team's given up or many they want to let him have this one last victory, but by the time the clock reaches 0:45, they lunge at him with barely any effort.

I'm screaming so loud my voice is becoming hoarse, and I know I'll sound like I've swallowed a box of nails tomorrow morning, but I don't care.

All I care about is that man out there, my fiance, who dives head-first over the scoring line with twenty-seconds left, doing a somersault roll and lying on his back, his chest heaving as the entire stadium erupts with glee.

I can feel the vibrations through my feet.

Corey staggers to his feet and high-fives everyone, his mud-streaked face glowing with happiness as his team gets into formation for the presentation of the trophy.

The announcer congratulates the Chargers on their win and hands the trophy, and the microphone, to a beaming Corey.

'I'd like to thank everyone for their support over the years,' he says, 'but most of all, I'd like to thank my fiancée, Alison Turner, the love of my life.'

The camera pans around to me, showing my glowing face on the huge screen. I wave my fingers in front of my face, showing off my engagement ring.

'Are you thinking about playing another year?' the announcer asks. He's a white-haired man who has to reach high above his head for it to hold the microphone so Corey can speak into it.

'Nah,' Corey says, smiling up into the stands. 'I'm ready to move on to the next chapter. Football was the centre of my universe for so long—now I'm ready for a new journey.'

My chest glows so much it feels like it's about to burst.

Corey and me. Me and Corey.

Exactly the way it should be.

20

EPILOGUE

ALISON

Five years later...

I'm still completely in love.

And how could I not be? Look at Corey, on the other side of the park, coaching a kids' football game. It's the under 10s side and the kids are panting around their mouth guards from sprinting up and down the field.

That's what Corey does now—when he's not building bespoke wooden furniture, he coaches kids' football. Our oldest son, Noah, has already decided he wants to be a football player, just like his dad, and he's tossing a toy football near the sideline.

I'm carrying Olivia and Emma trails behind me, grumpy at having to spend time with 'the boys'. Corey smiles and waves when he sees me and blows his whistle to announce training is over for the day, and the boys scatter back to their parents.

'How are my girls?'

He takes Olivia out of my aching arms and I can't

believe that after five years he can still anticipate everything I need.

'We're fantastic, aren't we?' I say to Olivia as I adjust her beanie. 'We had a great day at the princess castle.'

'Oh yeah?'

'Yeah.' I kiss him and it feels exactly the same as it always has—despite all those years, nothing's changed.

Except for one thing.

Corey doesn't know it yet, but baby number four is slowly growing inside me, and I've been waiting for the right time to tell him.

'Ew!' Emma says, turning away and pretending to throw up.

'Can we play football?' Noah shouts.

'Sure,' Corey says, as Emma groans. 'But only for five minutes, okay?'

21

EPILOGUE

COREY

Five years into our marriage and I still feel like I'm the luckiest man on earth. We're living in my house, with all three kids. My carved bed's got pride of place in my bedroom and Alison and I have slept on it ever since our wedding night.

The wedding itself was unbelievably beautiful, held in the valley behind the house with all of our family and friends. They were all there—how did I ever think anyone wouldn't support our relationship? Tess was the ring bearer, with the ring in a pouch on her collar, and she's still here now, sitting in front of us we drink tea on the balcony, her head resting on her paw.

The kids are inside with Alison's mother, giving us some much-needed time to ourselves.

Alison snuggles against my chest and plays with my shirt.

'How many copies of the book did you buy again?'

Her hair brushes against my cheek and I think about how many are in the box beneath my bed.

She finished my biography six months after we met, and

Caret Publishing eventually picked it up, selling more copies than I even thought possible, and I've got three first edition copies on our bookshelf, one for each the kids, each signed inside the front cover, plus those spare copies under the bed. Just in case.

It seemed to risky at the time, but I'm so grateful for the biography—it brought us together, and now it gives us a permanent record of the beginning of our relationship.

And it gave Alison a new career as a freelance writer—she's written biographies for three footballers, five Olympic athletes and a woman who survived for five years in the wilderness.

'I've got a few left.' With the angle she's sitting, I can see right down her cleavage, and I let my fingers explore her impossibly soft skin.

'Maybe you should pull them out,' she says. 'Sign another one.'

'Really?' I look down at her chocolate eyes and she smiles and places her hand over her stomach. We haven't exactly been careful, so it's not a total surprise, but at all the same, it feels like something that's been supposed to happen since the moment we met.

'Really,' she says.

I laugh and pull her on top of me. We kiss, and it's just as passionate as it's always been.

'How about we get inside and celebrate,' I say, pulling her close.

We walk inside together, arm-in-arm, and there's no doubt about it, Alison will always be my good luck charm.

ABOUT THE AUTHOR

Carmel Evans writes about curvy women and the alpha heroes who love them. Her stories are sweet, steamy and romantic, and she's a sucker for romantic movies, instant attractions and happily ever afters.

Watch out for more Carmel Evans stories coming soon!